HIS UNBURNED HEART

David Sandner

Published by Raw Dog Screaming Press
Bowie, MD
First Edition

Cover art copyright 2023 by Lynne Hansen
LynneHansenArt.com

Printed in the United States of America

ISBN: 9781947879768
Library of Congress Control Number: 2024932763

RawDogScreaming.com

Table of Contents

Also by David Sandner

Fiction

Hellhounds (with Jacob Weisman)

Mingus Fingers (with Jacob Weisman)

Scholarship

Critical Discourses of the Fantastic, 1712-1831

The Fantastic Sublime

As Editor

The Afterlife of Frankenstein

Philip K. Dick, Essays of the Here and Now

Fantastic Literature: A Critical Reader

The Treasury of the Fantastic (with Jacob Weisman)

For Amy, who might keep my heart in her desk drawer, if it, too, didn't burn.

His

Unburned

Heart

16 August 1822, Tuscany

Shelley's body on the pyre smoked, ruptured. Winding light round shadows, the fire moved and snapped and cracked—bright, shivering, shifting, glistening, spitting. Flames flared—yellow, pale green, numinous white, terrifyingly empty. Respiring in the wind off the sea, the fire heaved, staggered, loomed up, intolerable—laughing sharply, coughing smoke into a cerulean sky; the fire reached out to kiss our faces wet with sweat—as if we were its children. But we were nothing before that fire. My husband's funeral pyre on a beach near Viareggio.

Even before the burning, his body had been ruined: corrupted, half-eaten by the sea, with clothes tattered and once-flowing hair sparse and dun. Even before he was placed on the funeral pyre atop Trelawny's makeshift iron oven, the dried skin of his corpse had hung loose like an ill-fitting shift, patches sagging or furrowing as the Tuscan soldiers lifted the body from its shallow temporary grave of lime and sand on the narrow beach. When it burned, the skin along the face and legs, brittled by lime, blackened and cracked like parchment from an old book left unread for an age—a book of blasphemies to be put to the torch at last. The flames should have absolved us all—exchanging inevitable decay for nothing, releasing us, but, something would not give—

I felt I would choke but not from smoke—

His heart, unrecked, would not—

The fire keened in the wind. It barked, roared, whistled, inhabited by some daemon come to honor our dead prophet. When the body had burst into flame, it held shape still for a time, accepting the flames entwining it like a mummy. Until the burning cracked the bones, allowing the fire to worm in, greedily, and then the inner matter—already unintelligible as organs or muscle—bubbled thickly— sickeningly. And then—what then?

Unbearably, his heart would not—

At last, where there should have been only charred bone, nothing more, some…unknowable remained—more like an ideal thing from his dreams or poetry—as insistent as a conscience. There, in the revealed cavity of his cracked chest, lay his absurd heart: a dark lump, smoking.

Unaccountably, his heart—

Laid bare on blinding white sand before endless blue on a beach in Viareggio, his heart, immutable—

Shelley's heart would not burn.

There, in the charred lump of his unburned heart, in its impossibility, my story lies. If you will know it, you must know it with the unsayable left in; the excess, like his heart, abides.

Trelawny knelt close to the fire, closer even then Byron; shirtless, dripping sweat from his arms and off his thick beard, he raised his muscled arms in supplication. Shaking, wild-eyed, he seemed to want to throw himself into the flames. It was he who had insisted on burning the corpse. Reckless, high-spirited, a sailor and adventurer, Byron had christened him "my corsair" after the pirate hero of his poem—and Trelawny embraced the designation. He would, if he could lie enough and strive enough to live his life so. He had performed invented rites to honor the dead poet. He had poured wine and oils on the corpse, and on himself, and danced and recited ancient poetry to the sun.

Byron, in a tight black coat and breeches, remained close in, unmoving, burning coal eyes gazing into the inferno as if he had turned into a pillar of salt; the light hollowed his cheeks in his skull as he pursed in concentration.

A baker's dozen ill-attired Italian soldiers, a local militia, their white shirts soiled and untucked under indifferent brown longcoats, with overlarge hats scuffed and cocked hurry-scurry, moved away, murmuring, breaking what little discipline they had, milling nervously, turning their backs, crossing themselves.

"*The smell, the heat,*" they called to each other in Italian; "*the smoke,*" they said coughing, "*the devil's light!—the crazy English!*"

Their captain, his suit, though worn, in good discipline, looked pointedly out to sea at nothing. Nothing to notice, those were his unspoken orders: stand and endure.

In jealousy or frenzy at those who remained, the fire shot up astonishingly high and bright, intensifying, sparking, crackling, humming in the wind. The shimmering light hurt our witness eyes. Pulsing yellow in billowing white in flaring red, haloed in an orange luminescence, the fire cast our shadows on the sunlit beach. What is it we burned? What was my Shelley? With that fiery show, all stood dumb before the weird blaze, our bodies painted lurid colors, our faces changed for stranger's faces. Byron had endured the rituals with aplomb, somber at the circumstances but mildly amused at the worked up fervor of our self-appointed pagan priest Trelawney. The strange fire rising up cast his mood into deep shadow.

Leigh Hunt, the poet and publisher, and our friend, had come with Byron by the road—a dirt cartpath just off the narrow ribbon of sand before the sea. To the South lay Lerici, where my Shelley and I had lived at lonely Casa Magni, our boathouse hanging above the waves; to the North bustled Leghorn, which the Italians called Livorno, where Hunt had arrived from England and Shelley had sailed to greet him. Here, this beach…it was nowhere—a lost place (his last place) between here and there.

Hunt retreated from the heat, sagging in an attitude of grief against Byron's great black coach. A fancy script "LB" was inlaid in gold on the door that he opened. I stood behind the coach, though he did not note me as he stepped inside. For I was not there—I was in disguise; I had been disbarred from attending for I was only a woman (only Shelley's wife); I stood beside Tita, Byron's hulking manservant, who only frowned and bowed his head at all that transpired. Aside from the Italian militia, there were a half-dozen men manning Byron's boat, the *Bolivar*, rocking gently on the sea, close to shore. The boat had brought Trelawny and his iron oven for the pyre. The crew had lined the deck, holding absently to the rigging or leaning on the boat's edge, paying respect to the dead. Until the fire had brought wildness—frightening and terrible—to us all.

All marveled, but then averted their gazes from the heat. Their eyes became dulled to sublimity—who can look into its cracked-mirror gaze for long? Soon the Italians and Byron's sailors talked amongst themselves and paid no heed, waiting for the odd English nobles to finish their rites, waiting for normalcy to restore all illusions.

All had turned away, disturbed, afraid, except Trelawny, swaying, nostrils flared, wide-eyed, and Byron, unwilling to be moved by any power, any strangeness, wrapped in thoughts of fire to match the blaze before him. And me.

Then Trelawny saw the heart. His charlatan show over, no one watched him now. His display of pagan pomp served as a perfect distraction. Having been the center of attention, none watched him now, slightly embarrassed for him in his foolishness, slightly afraid of his audacity. Looking about himself first to see if any of the local militia watched, Trelawny snatched the heart out of his friend's cracked chest.

And no one else, not even Byron, saw—no one else but me: we two alone.

If the militia had seen him, he would have been quarantined, at least; what he had snatched out would have been quickly taken away. But then—what then? An unburned heart? What would they have done with it? Sailed it out to the deeps of the sea and thrown it in, fearful of contagion? Perhaps my Shelley's heart should be treated so—they would be right to fear it—for was it not, in its imperviousness, an indictment of us? What fragile hearts had we to judge anything?

Trelawny burned his hand badly in his rash act. He had moved quickly, but the heart itself was hard as stone, dark underneath but white with ash, smeared and crusted with hot matter—for a moment his hand smoked as it seared. Trelawny, however, mastered himself, not calling out, only stifling a keening sound that all let pass; they did not want to see anymore, or know anymore. He quickly wrapped his trembling hand in a cloth and hid the heart among his pagan appurtenances—the bottles, braziers, and incense he had brought with him to honor the dead poet.

Having snatched it from the fire, Trelawney lay my Shelley's heart, cooling, in a leather satchel. Why not? Shelley had no more need of it. One might take it as a remembrance of a loved one lost as one kept hair in a locket or took a finger bone. But this was something stranger. Why it endured was not the most important question. Instead, wonder: if Shelley left this tangible sign, who could read it? To whom did this sign, this wonder, this thing unprecedented—to whom did this unburned heart belong? If it had burned up, would we have been released from all our travails? Was his heart here to compel us to a task—what task? To give ourselves up to the fire? To abjure the flame and seek more life?

I do not know. But I ask you to remember: the heart is the reason before reason for all I relate. I would not turn away at any price from those flames. For there, in his heart, in its stubborn remainder, lie questions whose answers must be looked for inside other hearts, less impervious to flame, including my own.

So to my story.

2 August, Tre Pallazi de Chiesa, Pisa
(two weeks before the unburning)

Byron visited me in my grief and described to me the made-up rites Trelawney wanted to perform, foolishness cobbled together from old books he admired without understanding. Byron larked, with mild disdain, about it all but acquiesced to the overall idea, urging me to agree with it. Then he paused, and I knew, right in that moment, what came next: he would forbid me, when he could think of a way to say it. I could see the irresolution in his usually hardened gaze.

"But Mary…Maie," he said, trailing off, then more firmly: "You must not go to the cremation. It is not a fit place for a woman."

I did not reply.

"We shall have a memorial, later, that all can attend."

I said, "I shall speak with Trelawny—"

"He shall take my side. He plans pagan rites for the dead. Perhaps we shall have to dance naked as savages around the sacred flames—I do not know all his plans, but feel certain he will require you to stay away. The authorities of Italy will tell you the same, undoubtedly, for your safety from contagion. English custom agrees. I am simply—"

I grabbed at his hand, but he moved away from me.

"You and I know," I said, pleading when I wished not to, "the only contagion left on the corpse is death itself—which we have all caught and will succumb in time, no need to be separated from him for that."

I felt the heat of Shelley's burning already on my cheeks. I did not like the whine in my voice. I did not want to be in my own skin.

"And when have I been stopped by English custom?" I added. "When have you?"

"Nevertheless, it is decided." Byron turned away, as if the conversation had finished. He left quickly, closing the door as swiftly as he dared, taking no further leave. He feared me!

Rightly! I recalled when father laid down the law concerning Shelley—I must not see him anymore; I ran away to France, with him still married. That's what I think of the law laid down before me in such an imperious fashion. So Byron ordered me to stay. I suppose I should thank him for it, for I felt a rousing of my spirit from its low ebb. Life called me to it. My heart asked: am I not my mother's daughter?

16 August 1822, Mrs. Mason's House, Pisa
(the morning of the burning)

On the morning of Shelley's cremation, in the hour before sunrise, I stopped at the house of our friend, Mrs. Mason, where, in a private chamber, I posed like an artist's model before her looking glass. She stared into my face, lips pursed, humming deeply as she worked with make up to darken and coarsen my skin.

"You look," Mrs. Mason said absently, considering me with the attention one gives to the freshness of fish at the market, turning my face this way and that, wrinkling her nose, "much like her, your mother."

I blushed with pleasure at the comparison.

"Oh, none of that," she said, with humor, rocking back slightly in a short bark of a laugh, "I need to see your skin's true color if I am to make a man of you. The Italian sun has done its work, and that helps—male brutes are always so swarthy compared with us delicate…creatures." She turned and gazed up at herself in the mirror as if to carefully consider that word "beauty" in relation to herself, a mature woman who had known sorrow and joy. Time had jowled her face, paunched her body. But her pale eyes reflected her keen attention; she held her shoulders and chin with dignity; a wry smile showed her unafraid.

Mrs. Mason raised her eyebrows at herself skeptically—but she would let the assessment stand, her face seemed to say, regarding herself, as she did me, with humor but also with affection. She would take herself—she would trust her charms still. I longed for her confidence. I did not yet know if I could be equal to all that lay before me, even as I planned rebellion.

She looked down at my face again. "And your direct gaze, Mary, so inquisitive and acquisitive," she said, peering into my eyes, "the eyes that look through prating nonsense, they are your mother's particularly, and more than mannish enough for me!" She laughed. "They unnerve me, Mary! How many times your mother's gaze saw through me and my girlish fancies! In your gaze, I am fourteen again, and a fool!"

I felt a further stab of envy—Mrs. Mason had known my mother. Mary Wollstonecraft had been her governess; my mother had been able to act as more of a mother to dear Mrs. Mason then she could ever be to me. For only I survived my birth. I felt as well a jealous desire to keep Mrs. Mason close to me, perhaps as surrogate for what I had lost in my first unconscious days. And Shelley, my Shelley, had now joined my throng of lost ones. I did not speak but my breathing became ragged with conflicting emotion, and Mrs. Mason took my hand.

"And you must be still if I am to work," she said softly. I nodded. "To be a man, you must be more stern, and...," she shrugged, "unmoved. Though you go to mourn you must not show it. Remember, you are to be indifferent, callous.

"Think, Mary—all the world is yours now. Only women fret or swoon, having nothing else to do. When the world finally lays *them* low, as it does to all, men are indignant, surprised in their arrogance—women have been preparing for it their whole lives, knowing already that all is loss. If you will perform this ruse, be arrogant and assume the world."

She put her hand on my shoulder. I managed, at last, to speak.

"I'll try," was all I said, simply. My throat felt dry.

"Mrs. Mason" was not her name but a name she assumed from a figure in a children's story by my mother. Like the disguise I was now adopting, her name was put on. Mrs. Mason, like a man, assumed herself. She had been Margaret King when my mother first knew her. My mother, unsurprisingly, had made far too radical a governess for her father's taste and been dismissed—but not before she found a convert to the feminine call to freedom. The two had maintained a secret correspondence even after my mother's dismissal. Later, in deference to her family, Margaret King married the Earl Mountcashel, becoming the honorable Lady Mountcashel. It was not a good match. They argued; Lady Mountcashel would not be silent. She produced seven children, fulfilling her role in that way. But travelling in Rome she met George Tighe, her life's companion, and left her husband and dear children to stay with him in Italy. Her husband kept the children as law demands. With a shrug and open hand, Italy accepts us, the abandoned and scandal-ridden. Mrs. Mason gave up so much of value to become herself.

Mrs. Mason was formidable and imperious to detractors, self-contained and kind to friends. She lived a life chosen instead of taking what was left over—instead of only carving out some place inside other's choices as if one were a servant, or a dog picking scraps dropped from the table. With her companion Mr. Tighe, the self-invented Mrs. Mason had two more daughters, Nerina and Laurette.

Though she had never again seen her first children, it was not all loss, an important point.

Mrs. Mason returned to regarding my face, the skin between her eyebrows pinched in concentration.

"Men's faces are thicker than ours. But do not fret, many young men keep a boyish softness into their twenties," she said, talking more to herself as she made her way through her choices of brush and color and texture. "You will do, with a good hat, worn low like a young sharp. And I shall add some stubble to those cheeks."

"How did you learn to do this?" I asked quietly. She seemed so confident of this endeavor, one she herself suggested to me when I came to her in a rage because I could not attend my husband's funeral pyre for English custom, Italian law, and my husband's male friends working in concert. I had expected consolation; I had been led willingly into conspiracy. If only men could see Shelley's funeral, I would be a man, she had told me, and had taken me by the hand to lead me to her magic mirrors and wands of transformation to change the female frog into a young princeling. With sudden insight, I said: "You have been a man before." Obviously. I felt like the slow one at the party who finally, laboriously, works out the joke.

She smiled at me, leaned in, drawing my gaze with her own. In her eyes, I could see a cloudy reflection of myself, a shadowed face like a crescent moon.

"What woman who wants anything in life has not played the man?"

I smiled. She continued: "We must, after all, study our wardens for chances of escape! If only for a time! When I was young—younger," she said, putting her hand on my sleeve, her glance merry, "my figure had been less…rounded like a woman's than now." She regarded herself critically again. "Less matronly, in truth," she said with a theatrical sigh, "less this here, less that there. And I wanted to see the great medical lectures. The secrets of life being discovered by medical men—the secret springs in vitalism and galvanism, all that. And only men may hear of it! Are we not part of the world in which these secrets reside? For fear of our delicate natures, nature itself is hidden from us. So I became what I must become. I learned a great deal, about the wonders of modern medicine, the slovenliness of men, and the art of disguise."

She leaned back, as if a thought pushed her upright.

"But surely you have tried this?" I shook my head. "But how did you learn of all these things for your wild monster book? You have in it captured the problems, the possibilities, of our age. Did you not have some stratagem for access to the hallowed lecture halls of men? We women must be half-monster ourselves, sneaking around the edges, prying beyond our bounds...what was it? Yes, looking through the chinks of the wall from our closets at a world we cannot have, isn't that how the monster learns to talk? You must have had some way of getting into the halls of men?"

She looked expectant. I cleared my throat, parched as if I had taken sea water, but when I reached for words, they came in a torrent....

"Shelley and his nervous nature led us to learn more," I said. "We have often had to consult doctors, you know, for his health—that was part of our reason for coming to Italy. He and I used to especially talk together with one doctor, the celebrated Mr. Lawrence, about vitalism—the spark of life, and so much else. He was a master of the material scientific view and we respected him. We went to public lectures, where women could go—such as one by Mr. Andrew Crosse on electricity, in London. It was all on my mind. Then, when we came to Geneva and met Lord Byron...their talk was like alchemy, wild and mixing into the strangest things. Byron and Shelley, they were my theater where the experiments occurred," I said, the excitement of running away with Shelley, meeting the famous poet Byron, and an unseasonably wet summer in 1816 of laughter and talk at his Villa Diodati when all the world belonged to me, all of it I wanted—when I lived among the Elect as one of them—from that perfect state can there be anything but loss? Had there been anything but loss? "When Shelley and Byron first met they were like magnetized souls, drawn into incessant conversations of everything; each saw in the other...both an opposite and a match, like an impressive dark cloud lit by lightening. It was extraordinary, and I witnessed. I listened close."

I had tears in my eyes. I did not feel them come, but felt them hot on my cheek.

"I was so young, still half-girl. I did not know then how to speak to Byron, or if I ever could. But I was their audience—they performed for me. At night, in bed, Shelley and I would play the whole conversation again, animated, as if it were happening again, and I would speak to him as I could not with Byron, asking questions and making observations I could not share otherwise. The next day Shelley would repeat the best of what I said to Byron, and the conversation would go on to new dazzlements. I felt so...." I did not know what to say. "They spoke of the life within us, the experiments with electricity—spoke of everything, details, however morbid, nothing hidden or feared—they exposed the bodies and showed me, in their words, what might be possible; I saw it in my mind. And I saw what they should fear, my two wild men...and their fearlessness of the precipice!"

"Your two monsters," Mrs. Mason whispered. "You saw more than they could...."

"Yes," I said. My voice had risen in pitch. I brought it down, saying soft, "and you're right, I would have been half-monster if I could. I would be...."

Mrs. Mason nodded.

"You're ruining your disguise, however," she said, veering me away from despair with a kindly touch. There was in me something unresolvable. I caught a glimpse of it—as if below me a sudden cliff yawned, seen at the end of a walk, dimly through fog—a black ocean beyond; I let Mrs. Mason swerve me back to what remained to me—what I knew of myself. But it waited out there, always. A dark ocean. A moonless night. I belonged here, not there, I told myself, at least for now.

Mrs. Mason, with her steady eye that had known despair, looked on kindly, with an understanding that held me, like a sturdy rope lowered to a climber of the glaciered voids below Mont Blanc.

Her face seemed to say to me: it is not all loss, an important point.

"You are a remarkable liar," Mrs. Mason said. "Use this ability when you play your part. From conversations, from imagination, you made those wondrous strange things in your book?" she said, patting my tear tracks away with a puff, restoring her handiwork with quick work of pencils and brushes. She shook her head in wonder.

"That's the way," I said. I inhaled a long breath through my nose, straightened up, released everything. "As you well know, from your own work...."

Mrs. Mason had authored, like my mother, a children's book, *Stories of Old Daniel, or Tales of Wonder and Delight*. That's when she became "Mrs. Mason," her chosen pseudonym, from the name of the strict but loving governess in my mother's children's stories.

"Oh, they were nothing," Mrs. Mason said, pursuing her lips. They had been, in point of fact, successful enough to span a sequel. "Just stories to amuse children."

"I sometimes think children," I said, "despite their reputation for incredulity, harder to 'take in' then adults. If you do not imagine with a child's heart, without reservation, they will turn away from you to other amusements; adults are desperate for relief and willing to give attention to any sensational thing. I should like to try my hand at a children's story."

"If you decide to, Laurette would love to hear it! As would I!" she said, tucking my hair behind my ear so she could work along the sides of my face. "But *your* story made me believe terrific things—things I knew might be in our reach in the fullness of time. I trembled. Now I find it was not only written by a slip of a girl, and one who did not see the experimenters in their scientific theatres, cutting and shooting electricity through the dead—no!—this girl caught up only words dropped before her. You make me think the world can be made up of only words!" She laughed.

Isn't it? I thought. Something made me resist saying it. For that was a private thought too monstrous to be given breath. One might say it easily enough, perhaps, for attention in a literary salon, to make the other bluestockings laugh—but to believe it, as I did, was more dangerous than a salon wit realizes. All the world would turn then, on the right word, or the wrong one. *And didn't it?*

"Haven't you made up your life of well-chosen words," I said, with a placidness I did not feel. "Your name is a fiction—well chosen, I think! Do you not make your story in despite of others?"

Like Mrs. Mason, I, too, had chosen my life when I had run away with Shelley. He had been, like she was, already married. I had lived with someone already married for happiness' sake. I had taken a name that was, at that time, a fiction: "Mrs. Shelley." Only later, after his first wife's death, did we marry, and I became the "real" Mrs. Shelley, sometimes called "Author of *Frankenstein*." The reviewers thought a man must have written the anonymously-published *Frankenstein*; it must be Shelley, they claimed! I wrote it! I wrestled, restless, with my bedding at night, my story haunting my dreams. The rudeness of the question so often asked, "but you—*you* wrote it?" I was the one who pressed on when the ghost story contest dried up for "my two monsters" and they wandered away to tour the Alps. I was the one would not be stopped. The story swelled in me.

I needed that determination again, though I had lost my guiding star, my Shelley. My last words to him had been recrimination, spoken out of my loneliness and isolation at Casi Magni. But I would not be stopped now. I would mourn my loss, my failings; I would celebrate my time among the Elect. My precious time with my Shelley.

And I *would* see my husband's cremation.

Did I not run away with him, to France, and beyond? When my stepmother came over to France to retrieve us, we lounged in our radicalism, redolent of insouciance and too much red wine. I did *not* go home. We sent Claire out to talk to her, laughing—and then on we went to Geneva, and finally, when we had the funds, to Italy. When the French Revolution had burst and raved, where did my mother go? A writer then—no more a governess of children—she was there, where she needed to be, excited by liberty, living, contending with Burke, and anyone. When I am afraid of my own desires to break free, when I think of all I will lose for my freedoms, all the fires burning my dearest possessions one by one, I think on her and I am resolved still.

Mrs. Mason had moved on to my hands, turning them over as if buying new gloves from a dubious seller, doubtful if there was value there but considering what she might be willing to pay, in a pinch, for them.

"We must make them look rougher," she said, "more used and coarse. Especially on the back, where one might see them."

Mrs. Mason pulled my hair back, clipping it so my hair hung loose in a man's fashion down my neck. "It will do," she said, "it will do when we have a good cap on it. Now let me see that expression of arrogance."

I mimed sternness. She laughed.

"No, no, I'm sorry—it will do!" I laughed with her. Could I ever grow into being her in time? How had she handled the losses she bore? Her seven children, not dead but severed from her? Did she have a cliff inside her, waiting down the end of a foggy road—a path that did not turn but ran straight over and down to a black sea? Terrible to say, I hoped she did, because then there was hope for me.

She drew a finger over my brow and down the side of my cheek. Something soft entered her imperious artists' gaze.

"Never," Mrs. Mason said, her eyes focusing, "did I see him look happier than the last glance I had of his countenance."

She had told me she had seen him—Shelley—when I had come to her in my desperate, fruitless search for him after his shipwreck. He had visited and they had chatted of nothing. On the Monday he was lost, she woke to find she had dreamed of him. Mrs. Mason had dreamt that she was somewhere, she knew not where, and Shelley came looking very pale and fearfully melancholy. She said to him, "You look ill. You are tired. Sit down and eat."

"No," he had replied. "I shall never eat more; I have not a *soldo* left in the world."

"Nonsense," she said, "this is no inn—you need not pay—"

"Perhaps," he answered, "it is the worse for that."

Then she awoke and going to sleep again she dreamt that my Percy was dead and she awoke crying bitterly and felt so miserable. She was so struck with these dreams that she mentioned them to her servant the next day—saying she hoped all was well with us.

"You must go to the pyre," she had said, after recounting the story to me. "It is your right, by heaven, if not by men."

Mrs. Mason completed her art, preparing her canvas as promised. Getting to Shelley's funeral had been my contribution. We had thought at first that I must try to hire a coach and be "passing by"—a wonder struck traveler who halts to see a poet's cremation. But I would be too conspicuous, too much a figure to be gawked at. The disguise would prove too thin. I must be someone unlooked for, a part of the scenery, the equipage.

"Would Trelawny help?" Mrs. Mason had asked. "You could come in Byron's boat with the thing he built—the iron oven—and the fuel for the pyre?" She looked uncomfortable at the thought of

Trelawny's grotesque spectacle. "You could be a young sailor and watch from the sea?"

I shook my head.

"His manliness would balk—he would not credit my nerves to hold up. And I believe he would see me as intruding in a man's privilege. Besides, the water might prove very bad indeed for your handiwork!"

I clapped my hands.

"A servant," I said, "a footman, on Byron's coach."

Mrs. Mason looked at me as if I were a prestidigitator, pulling one bird after another out of my sleeves.

"Brilliant!" she said. I felt, for a moment, that I deserved to be the celebrated "Author of *Frankenstein*."

"I know what to do," I said. And could not resist theatrically putting my finger to my lips. She had nodded. We smiled together, conspiratorially.

I had rushed to see Byron's right hand man, Giovanni Battista Falcieri, known as Tita, calling him down to a servant's door on a narrow Pisan side street, a rank alleyway of grey stone walls rising up three stories with broken, uneven cobblestones below fit to turn an ankle in the uncertain light. Tita arrived, cleaning his hands with a rag as if he had been eating, looking at me with a puzzled expression.

"Si, Signora Shelley?" he asked sympathetically to the heartbroken widow. I could see in his eyes he wondered if I had lost my senses in my grief, had come to the wrong door or lost my way home. I used this sympathy to my advantage. Ruthlessly.

"Dear Tita, my friend," I said. "I need your assistance."

He said, as I had hoped he would say, what he should not have said. Unthinkingly, he declared, "anything for you, Signora Shelley." All chivalry.

He would not have been able to resist my plan, anyway, even before that manly declaration. When Shelley and I arrived in Italy, we had come thinking to meet in the flesh our horrendous notions of blood-thirsty banditti, cruel Counts, and scheming monks from the Gothic sensation novels of Mrs. Radcliffe and "Monk" Lewis and others. Did not every Italian beggar hide a stiletto, every aristocrat a cunning scheme, every convent a kidnapped beauty? So Byron loaned us his own bodyguard, the fearsome Tita Falcieri, for a time. We felt safe: he had both a good command of English and a fearsome demeanor.

"His face alone," Byron laughed, striking the hulking Italian on the arm, "frightens off the banditti. But you may trust him with your life—he has sworn a blood-oath to me."

Tita was a massive man with a broken face. His shoulders stretched across his black shirt. He wore short pants with great baggy pockets in which he hid weapons, as we soon discovered. His smile showed blackened teeth in his sunburnt face. He looked the very embodiment of Gothic terrors.

"He was my gondolier, in Venice," Byron said, as if that were reason enough to trust his knowledge of Italian intrigues, moonlight rendezvous, and deadly secrets. Byron's numberless and dangerous love trysts from that time are legend, even among the Venetians, who pride themselves on their sangfroid.

Our fears of Italian bogeymen dissipated in the Italian sunlight, and soon actual Italians, living easy lives, replaced our fantastic notions of assassins and secret tribunals.

Yet, when we asked Tita one day, "Are there really banditti in the woods?"

He answered, "In many places, on the campagna before Rome, yes."

"Do you have a stiletto?"

He showed us the fearsome Italian weapon, producing it by some sleight of hand from some hidden pocket of his baggy pants. He held it out for us a moment before making it disappear into the folds of cloth again.

"It looked stained," Shelley later said, with a shiver. Of course, he liked to scare himself.

Shelley never got over fearing Tita, though always less then he feared the banditti. But Tita, to my surprise, took an instant liking to me. It was again that dreadful book of mine. How it does seem to creep inside them all!

After we had settled in, and Shelley had left me behind, feeling safe enough to explore Pisa without Byron's bodyguard, Tita had made a confession.

"Signora Shelley," he had said. "I am pleased to meet you. I am your Frankenstein!"

"Like the doctor?" I asked, guessing at his confusion, having run into this problem before, but letting him sort it out for himself.

"No, no, the creature, the outcast—I am the monster." He thumped his chest.

Astonishing! How many men see themselves reflected in that dark mirror? I would have to start keeping count.

"Thank you," I said, warmly. "But how—?"

"Lord Byron commented—I asked to read it. He graciously permitted. My reading English is not so great: I had one of the other servants, a student, who knew how, read it to me. I remain entranced. You see into life and death. I am your…literary admirer."

By his deliberate pronunciation of the final phrase, he marked it as unfamiliar, recalling it from somewhere…perhaps from Byron or his student friend? He has remained my "literary admirer." Shelley could see I trusted him and tried to warn me off.

"I am certain he has murdered at least two men," Shelley said, "Byron said so." Shelley had recounted two hideous stories of cut throats, trying to frighten Claire and me; Claire had been wound up, wild-eyed around Tita ever since. But I would not turn from my creature like the good doctor did to his. I did not doubt, as a gondolier, he had cause to use his stiletto in anger, and perhaps, as Byron's or another's guard, in professional service, but I sensed in his broken face a firm conviction—with Tita, one was either in or out of some magic circle; perhaps he had done terrible things to those without the invisible line he drew. But I was in and would always be so and he would never hurt me. I simply knew it, and had never had cause to question it. Call it woman's intuition if you must. Or simply trust the woman who saw into life and death and wrote a terrible book about monsters. I should know the difference between one kind of monster and another, if anyone should.

I told Tita what I required. A place as a footman at the back of Byron's immense carriage, where I knew Tita himself would be riding, overseeing everything. He would have to compromise his service to Lord Byron or contravene his promise to me, his literary admiree. He burst into tears.

I felt contrite and hid my smile as much as I might behind a hand as I consoled him. Of course, he gave everything I asked: a boy's footman costume, a place on Byron's ornate carriage. What choice did he have?

The day before the burning of Shelley's body at Viareggio, our friend Edward Williams had been cremated on a nearby beach. As luck would have it, a boy of about my height and build accompanied Byron's carriage. Hadn't he already been looked at? If anyone were to notice the footman, would it not be on the first day?

My Ned, my noble confidante, was a Navy man, an experienced sailor. If they were to be saved, Ned would have been the one to do it. Shelley loved sailing but would learn nothing, relying on others, not caring to apply himself to anything practical like learning to swim though he loved boating.

I later heard that when Ned's body had been uncovered, Byron exclaimed, "Is that a human body?"

He had held his handkerchief up to his nose.

"Why it is more like the carcass of a sheep, or any other animal, than a man: this is a satire on our pride and folly."

16 August 1822, on a beach near Viareggio
(just before the burning)

After I had taken my place on the great carriage, and we had drawn it around to the front of Byron's great Palazzo Lanfranchi, Leigh Hunt, mourning in rumpled black clothes, mis-matched and worn, emerged to attend the proceedings. He stooped, walking with weary steps—he never even glanced at me as he stepped into Byron's ornate coach. A moment later Byron followed, dressed smartly in black finery, tight, straight pants and vest; he walked quickly to the carriage and I thought I had fooled him, too, when he jumped up and ducked his head in. But he drew his head out and stood up fully on the step.

Byron let his gaze slide until he met mine. I thought of looking down, but that seemed even worse.

"This is no merry undertaking," he said, the pun for my benefit. "Are you sure, boy, that you are up to it?"

I did not trust myself to speak. I nodded.

He lifted himself up enough on the runner to see Tita, his manservant, holding to the other side of the carriage back. "I trust you will see that everyone remains…in hand?"

Tita, looking embarrassed, gave a short bow. Byron knew I had enlisted the help of his man—and I regretted the trouble I had caused dear Tita. No one could have gotten so close to Byron without Tito allowing it: he was bodyguard and nursemaid. I had opportuned on friendship.

"Then let us set the world on fire," Byron said angrily, ducking his head into the carriage.

I nodded, overcome by emotion.

So I went, only to lose Shelley's heart, that deformed thing of beauty, to Hunt.

After the pyre burned down, as if Shelley's unburned heart were but coins in his purse that would go, of course, to the thief who rifled the corpse first, Hunt claimed the impossible prize. Trelawny had placed it in his leather satchel, and tucked it among his jumble of pagan paraphernalia. I watched him from where I stood at attention, like Tita, as an accouterment of Byron's ostentation. Sweat itched beneath my livery. My neck felt raw, chaffed. It was no small thing, I discovered, to be a servant—to not be able to step into the shade where and when I would. I'd thought I'd understood, intellectually, but that turns out to be worth nothing when you have an itch you may not scratch—from such small denials is humiliation inculcated in the lower classes.

Trelawny had risen unsteadily to his feet. I don't know how he stood it. The heat, even at a distance, blasted my face as the weird fire pulsed—even as it burned down, still a too-bright orange bursting out of a near dark purple center. No longer rising over us, it still cracked fierce and dominating, shaking and swaying like the witches waiting on Macbeth to ask forbidden questions so they could riddle him his doom. I moaned in grief, but the rushing of the fire covered everything.

Trelawny backed away—his wounded hand bound, the heart in his bag clutched in his other fist. Closest to the fire, he had refused to yield to it until it offered him something—perhaps helping him conjure the unburned heart like a necromancer of old, or more like an alchemist working gold to discover immortality. Trelawny's chest was bare, wet with sweat. His wild hair and beard seemed living things, snakes writhing in the awful heat and wind. He looked around, holding the bag with the heart uncertainly.

I thought to call out to him, to call him to his Mary. I could impose: give me the heart! I would weep and he would yield it, manfully.

But I was *not there*.

If I spoke, Tita would pay the price, and I could not have that.

I guessed what Trelawny was going to do next. He would show off his miraculous prize. He was Trelawny—a storyteller, a dreamer, yes, and a liar, who wished to share whatever showed him to be a wonder; the heart was proof that he had withstood the heat beyond all others and had alone returned to tell the tale. He had been where he most wanted to be, the place where life itself seemed to quicken, full of meaning.

Trelawny would have shown Byron first, of course, but Byron was already moving away toward the water. He had begun to remove his coat to swim out to sea. Fletcher, his long-suffering valet, anticipating the desire, already stood on the shore, stiffly erect, his ankles wet from the highest waves that stretched themselves out below them, his arms out to receive his Lord's castoffs. Out on the water, the *Bolivar* rocked gently. The day before, Trelawny told me, Byron had swum out from the beach after Ned's funeral rites, only to cramp up and vomit. Trelawny told it as if concerned for Byron, as if merely sharing a worry about a friend, but the gleam in his eye betrayed his satisfaction. Trelawny could not help competing with Byron, though a man of Byron's accomplishments would often show him up. And a man of Byron's temper would make sure Trelawny knew he had been shown up. Of course Byron would need to have another go. Neither man's pride could resist a challenge.

Trelawny turned and looked at Byron's back a moment. Then he walked to Leigh Hunt, standing not far from me by the carriage. Hunt had stood with his hands clasped, rocking in misery; he might have been praying but he looked to me as if he were vexed, perhaps about his lost magazine going up in the fire (for that was why he had come to Italy, at Shelley's request, to publish something new and radical beyond the reach of English censorship laws), though Byron still promised to give him something to publish in it. And I did as well. I suppose he knew that Byron might yet change his mind.

On first arrival at the rising pyre, Hunt had moved toward it with a kind of bustling determination, joining Trelawny as he lit the fire. The flames had chased Hunt back to a safe distance. He seemed to note more acutely, with nervous glances, and runnings of his hands through his thinning hair, the disgusted reactions of the Italian militia. Byron and Trelawny ignored the watchers as long as they did not interfere. Perhaps Hunt feared each of the militia men would take notes and sell a version of what happened here before he could.

Opening the bag, Trelawny's strange find received from Hunt the attention of a newborn brought to a doting grandparent. Hunt exclaimed in wonder at it. He seemed to try to cry, to shake himself as if he sobbed. Then he begged for it. Promised in some sort of oath to take care of it. I couldn't have done it better myself. Trelawny looked confused.

"I thought to give this to…" Trelawny said. To me! Obviously. But Trelawny could not resist an oath—a manly oath under suppressed emotion. The outcome, as Hunt calculated, was inevitable. Trelawny seemed to gather himself, to throw out his chest and stand firmly with legs apart, one arm crooked behind him like a schoolboy about to recite his lesson at the board.

"Here," he said, handing over the satchel. "Treat it like…" Trelawny sought the metaphor "…wings…from heaven." Not well done. It would have to do.

I started forward but Tita grabbed my arm and shook his head.

His wide, squashed face was close; I darted a look into his

fearsome black eyes. He looked at Byron and back at me. I remained in my place.

"What have you there?" Byron said, come up from the waves. He stood behind Trelawny and Hunt, his shirt partway unbuttoned to show another shirt tucked underneath. He had more clothes than a lady has undergarments.

All three men exclaimed over it; they wondered at it; they envied it of each other. Byron asked to hold it and Hunt could not refuse. Byron looked at the charred remain, then his eyes flicked up to meet mine. He frowned.

"Do not lose it," he said, loudly.

"I would not," Hunt said, taking it again as if offended.

He wasn't talking to Hunt. Trelawny looked at him strangely. Byron put his hand on Trelawny's shoulder.

"Get me the skull, then, man," he said, "and after we will try our strength in the waves, swimming out to the *Bolivar*."

Trelawny returned to the fire, which had calmed, but the skull had cracked, or Trelawny cracked it in the attempt to retrieve it. There is a story that Byron drank from a skull in his youth, but I like to think he would not use Shelley's skull so—or if he did, that he would drink only the nectar of heaven from it. Trelawny knew the story, too, and perhaps made his own decision about it. After, as the fire slowly subsided even further, becoming only normal flame again, the two men waded into the ocean; the blue waters, calm now, bore them up easily as they treaded over the top of its vastness.

So I lost his heart. I stood watching as Leigh Hunt held it, clutching it to his chest. I stood at my position behind the carriage, waiting. I had become a man to be here, but could do nothing to help myself. I told myself to breathe. I vowed to get the heart back. I made myself turn away from Hunt and watch Byron and Trelawny arrive at the *Bolivar*. A wine bottle was handed down to them in the water.

They treaded water, trading swigs. They laughed at some ridiculous manly joke. I wanted to dunk them both under for Byron's knowing I was here and allowing me to be outmaneuvered by Hunt.

Leigh Hunt was a maddening problem of a man. Average height, ruddy faced and slovenly, he was young, only in his thirties, but seemed already bent with age. He had published Shelley and given him the best notice of his career. He had been my friend. He would publish my work. But he took the heart without considering me; no, it was worse than that: like the others, even not knowing I was there, he had thought of me, yet—somehow I knew already—he did not think I deserved the heart. I did not think I did, either; but he was not the one to tell me so—and there is the distinction on which I made my vow: I would have it!

If I had been a man, perhaps a duel would have followed as the most direct way to what I wanted. Byron was a crack shot. But I would need another way.

Byron and Trelawny came slowly back, bobbing over the swells. Trelawny would watch the fire burn down and gather the ashes for burial. He would travel toward Livorno on the *Bolivar* with his oven and Shelley's remains. Byron and Hunt, with Shelley's heart, would ride back in Byron's coach to Pisa. Holding tight to the back, I rode with them into town. I was tired but shaking with emotion as we jutted and rocked. We slowed near a final turn before arriving at Byron's home and Tita said, "now, go!" I looked at him, confused; he turned his hand up, furious, and whispered, "jump, little fire!"

I looked at him a moment longer, muttered a thanks and jumped, running back to my house, not caring if anyone saw me or recognized me. I stepped in through a side door where I had Catarina, my servant, waiting. My time as a servant made me conscious enough of what she had done so casually in waiting that I thanked her, which only confused her. I changed as quickly as I dared. I learned later I still had a smear of grease paint on my forehead, as if to add to my air of insanity when I confronted Hunt. But at that moment, for me, time was all.

As I moved through the hallways toward the front parlor, I called to my two housemates, my stepsister Claire and Ned's wife Jane. It had been an open secret between us where I had been that day, so they came quickly from other parts of the house with questions I barely heard. They came through two doorways suddenly, Claire more casual in a blue dress tied with ribbon high around her waist, skirt slim, long and columnar, her black hair pinned back loosely so strands fell across her face; Jane wore a French patterned frock that hung in folds decorated with little bows along the outer crease and her hair had been tightly wound, with light brown ringlets perfectly framing her shining eyes and little mouth. They both looked at each other as I failed to respond to their questions.

"What's wrong?" Jane asked.

"You must come," I asked, taking both their hands. "I need you now."

With a whirlwind of gathering coats and shoulder shawls and hats, shouting to Catarina and to Jane's woman to fetch this or tie that, we swept out of the house and crossed the bridge over the Arno to Byron's Palazzo. I hastily told them about the fire and the heart and Hunt. They made noises of sympathy; Claire added welcome grunts of ire. I liked to think one of them told me about the grease paint but I just wouldn't listen. The smear marked my head like Cain's marked him out as outcast into dark emotion he could not repudiate.

Leigh Hunt met me at the doors to his suite of rooms on the ground floor of Byron's Palazzo.

"My deepest condolences," he said. He bowed to me. He still wore his tired black out-of-style coat, unbuttoned now to show his mis-matched vestcoat beneath that proved, on inspection, to be a more faded shade of black: he had, it seemed, bought a new outer coat—and that sometime in the past—and conserved the vest. Such was the sorry fate of a publisher of radical poets.

Behind him, I could see Marianne in her house clothes, with three of her children, Thornton and two of the younger ones—Swinburne and Percy (as in Percy Bysshe Shelley Hunt!)—around her skirts. Young Swinburne was tying himself in her apron strings. I raised my hand to her, for we were—I thought—friends. She gave me a peculiar look.

"Thank you." I paused, sensing the awkwardness between us, "Mr. Hunt," I said, then added after a painful pause, "Leigh."

Seeing me motion to Marianne, he looked back and saw the object of my glance. He stepped out and closed the door behind him, as if I were a stableboy looking impertinently at his wife. It floored me even more to think, surprised: he expected this! He knew I would come for it and still he took it first. His eye had a contrition inexpertly masking resolve.

"I," I did not know what to say, "I have come looking for Shelley's heart." I said it without the conviction I had meant to, as if I lodged a mere request.

"It is safe," Hunt said firmly. "I assure you…Mary, I will honor it." He opened his door and backed in. "Now, pray, excuse my alacrity at taking leave—it has been a long two days—terrible—I need rest. And you! Surely, you should look to your affairs—"

"No, no," I said, putting my hand out on the closing door. "I will have the heart," I said, with more conviction. He would not even invite the grieving widow in! It was too much altogether.

He "tsked." To my face. Twice. He would not meet my gaze now. He clasped his hands, hunched his shoulders, inhaled through his nose, pursued his lips, gazed at some spot on the flagstones, making uncertain noises as if working himself up to give me news of bad marks in school.

"Shelley's heart is…," he said, shaking his head, theatrically regretful, "too great, you know."

I put a hand on his sleeve, plucking at it twice in my compressed state of agitation.

"Too important to leave to his widow?" I wished to catch his eye; he would not have it. Some say my curious eyes, changeable of color between brown and blue, somehow not just either, would mesmerize and compel. Had Hunt heard tell of my glittering eye?

"Oh, yes, yes," he took out a handkerchief, causing my hand to drop from his arm; he covered his eyes a moment, an odd gesture of overwhelm. But he continued differently. He shoved the handkerchief in his pocket. He had settled on a voice he felt comfortable with now: a husband giving orders.

"Understand. It belongs to the world. Shelley would want it so. I am his publisher…his friend…it falls to me to make his name. He will be recognized for the great poet he…was, Mary. Leave this to me. Mark me. This is best."

"I am not," I paused, biting off the words, "your wife."

Hunt stammered, his face reddening: "of course not."

"Shelley is my husband. I will have…."

"Now see here," he said. "You should assign all rights to me. His reputation will be cared for, his works loved by someone who…."

How had we turned to talking of Shelley's poems and other writings? He frowned. I frowned in return. What was it about the heart that he wanted? A last relic of the poet who was to help him with his new magazine? A remainder of a dream he had had, now crumbling? Would his magazine, *The Liberal*, continue beyond the first issue or two, once Byron's help, without Shelley to keep him to the sticking point, dissipated? Was the heart a tool to future endeavors, something to show the up and coming writers, to inspire them and ensure their trust? Something to show potential backers of his next literary exertion to prove his value to literature? He scrunched up his eyes and mouth as if tasting something sour. What did he see when he saw me—a poor widow—before him?

I said, "I will care for them…."

"I read your letter, Mrs. Shelley, your horrible letter, the one you sent me."

He balled his fists, shaking them up and down like a performer miming running in his excess of feeling. He had let it out at last… the cat departed the bag. I stopped up short, stricken. Please, please, no, I thought, let me never have written it. I felt blind, dizzy. The letter I had sent, full of recriminations, full of anguish—the letter I regretted, poured out of my loneliness at Casa Magni, bitterly imploring Hunt to make Shelley listen to me. I repented all I said about hating our isolation and hating, too, Shelley's love of our isolation. I thought I had been sending it to our friend: I had sent it, I saw now, to Shelley's friend. I was mortified about my last words to my Shelley—I could never take them back—but that was my shame, not his to exploit!

"You made yourself clear, Mrs. Shelley. I do not relish being the one to speak plainly; you should know these things. But our Shelley needs it said. You could not stand by him in life. You should do what he needs now. I'm sorry to say it: You and Shelley, and me…and Byron, too, we have lived scandals. But a woman can't do that. You can't speak for him now. None will listen. I know it's not fair, but think of Shelley…think of him for once and what is best for him." He had been untracked, speaking in great earnest, looking along the cracks of the flagstones again for inspiration when he looked up into my face and what he saw made him flinch. He stepped back and closed the door in my face abruptly.

I will not tell you what was in my face, for I had no mirror. I should have been abashed; I could have crawled away, scuttling, under a rock below the deepest green sea, where my Shelley had died. Instead, a vent below the ocean spewed lava, boiling the seas, blotting the heavens with smoke, and remaking the world. He saw it on my face and ran for cover. I would now be not a man again, nor a woman either, for that matter—but a monster of my own creation: myself!

After a pause, I flung myself at his door, pounding on it:

"Your heart will burn," I cried, "you have none—it will burn, Hunt! Hunt!"

Claire came up behind me and threw her arms around me.

"Shhh," she soothed, "Not that way."

"He said—"

"I heard him—all of Pisa heard his bile. He cast his words to the winds, where the gossip will fly to all ears. If it were me I would scratch out his eyes—which I recommend—but only when there is no door between you and him."

I clung to Claire. We looked at each other. She gave me a cat smile, full of mischief. Then she laughed, and I smiled sadly, though I was shaking. Claire was always there to madden me, to scare me, to run ahead of me, to fall behind, to ruin my plans, to make me weep, to test me, to find me wanting, to leave me lonely, to believe in me. She was my thorn, my stepsister.

"This is beastly," Jane said, from behind Claire. "I will talk to him. Don't you worry, Mary. I will do it."

"Talk? I don't plan to talk." We all stood a moment. "I will go to Byron. They live in his house—he will help me."

Claire released me. "I will not go up to him, or even wait. You must go on alone."

Far too much history between them.

I looked at Jane. "No," she said. "I will stay and get in to talk to Hunt. You will see."

I didn't want her help convincing him. I wanted a club to hit Hunt on the head. He would see something then. Stars that called out his name, perhaps, and a blackness from the corner of the night sky infesting his distempered brain.

When I went upstairs, I received no satisfaction. Byron was indifferent—maddeningly indifferent. Hadn't he told me not to lose the heart? Wasn't that message directed to me? Mercurial Byron could be generous to a fault, then turn and refuse help on the least pretense; rather, he followed some code that seemed to run moral calculations that he then followed scrupulously—inhumanly so, making him seem to run hot or cold, all care and attention or only haughty disdain.

After knocking on Byron's door and bursting past a servant when it opened, I took the stairs two at a time, holding my dress bunched before me. At the landing, Byron's dog, Moretto, looked at me, breaking into a fearsome grin, breathing loudly, wagging its tail twice, thumping it loudly on the floor without rising. Fletcher, coming out of one door, put his hand up to hold me off, and stepped to another door; knocking twice and opening it, he announced me immediately, as if I were expected. Perhaps I was. I came in behind Fletcher into Byron's study. Byron was writing poetry. Dressed in an elegant oriental dressing gown, complete with silk hat and his fancy shoes turned up at the end, with tassels, he held the pen up at moment before returning it to its inkwell. It was perhaps not the best time. I stammered something by way of greeting. Byron looked bemused. Why had I come? What did I expect? Byron leaned back and made a motion of his hand, both dismissing Fletcher and bidding me go on and say what I had come to say. What had I come to say? I had come to him as I would have come to my Shelley; but it was not the same. I articulated my outrage at Hunt's claim on Shelley's heart.

Byron pursed his lips, then shrugged; he'd known this. Wearily, he said, "Are there not more important things? Your welfare, your child's? I had wanted the skull but it was not to be. Hunt could have been more thoughtful but then he would have had to be a thoughtful man instead of Hunt. *C'est la vie,*" he said with studied ennui.

I begged to differ; rather, I wished I begged to differ. I cannot tell you what I said. I babbled, shaking my hands to illustrate my breaking heart. After watching me like an audience member at a performance, Byron shook his head. This play would not have a long run. He made a motion, dismissing me.

Holding my clenched hands together to stopper myself from speaking, I withdrew.

"And, Mary," he said. I turned back to him, pivoting stiffly like an automaton. "You have something on your forehead. Here," he said, indicating by touching his own head.

I reached up and found the greasepaint, smearing it on my fingers. I tried to speak but stammered to a stop. I closed the door and fled.

How had I come to this? I should have known better. Had Byron been waiting for this interchange since our former conversation when he had forbade me to go to the funeral, or perhaps since he noted me clinging, leech-like, to the back of his carriage?

But perhaps Byron knew I would balk? Perhaps Byron's stratagems run deeper, have more layers then I had guessed at the time? Byron had said "no" to my attendance at the funeral, and I attended; now he refused to help me retrieve Shelley's unburned heart, and so I would have it. I learned later that after our interview, Byron had assigned Tita to watch over me. Tita said the exact words were, "you set this fire; you tend the flame." Not an endorsement, not even necessarily positive, but not clearly negative. And Byron knew what Tita would do: he would help me in whatever way I demanded. My literary admirer, what else could he do? Perhaps Byron was daring me to be more, to be a monster, to be the unstoppable Mary Wollstonecraft Shelley. So be it.

17 August 1822, Byron's great Palazzo Lanfranchi, Pisa—night (a day after the burning)

In the evening, Claire and I came by alleys and byways, the longways around as if assassins and spies followed us, to Byron's Palazzo. Two women should not go out by night alone; so Tita escorted us. He had eyes to see that we were not dressed like two ladies. But his approach seemed to be to pretend as much as possible that he had no idea what was going on, and that we were on an evening walk.

I was dressed in a simple dark blue dress, full cut for easy movement. The darkness of the frock would help conceal me.

Whispering in my ear, Claire, in high spirits, said: "If they catch you, tell them you're sleepwalking."

I rolled my eyes theatrically.

"Yes, because I can talk while I sleepwalk...?"

"Tell them you're insane, who wouldn't see that must be true?"

"I'll tell them my sister drove me to distraction."

Claire dressed like a pirate, black breeches and cap pulled low. A white loose shirt (of Ned's, I thought sadly), and a blue sash across her chest. On seeing us for the first time, Tita put his hand over his mouth to prevent comment, or perhaps laughter. He simply bowed and remained silent. As we traversed the alleys of Pisa, we kept to shadows. The night watch might have thrown us in the Arno and asked questions later, for we looked like what we were: up to no good.

Tita opened a servant's door of the Palazzo Lanfranchi; he agreed to let Claire in by the front, while he would wait outside by the river

Arno to escort us back, shortly, we hoped—home again, with my husband's heart clutched to my bosom. Claire's part (as always, I thought uncharitably) was distraction, if needed. Byron, who had boarded the Hunts for Shelley, had grown to hate the Hunt children and had taught his dog, Moretto, to growl and harry them. He left the bull-mastiff at the top of the staircase from the floor where the Hunts stayed to his apartments upstairs so that he could write poetry in peace. Claire knew the beast and was to bring it down, and set it to barking if I whistled. But if all was well, I was to come out Hunt's front door so we could make our escape together.

I am cognizant that it wasn't much of a plan. In my defense, the plan sounded better in the moment then written here in hindsight. When Tita and I had walked into the soot black of the alley beside Byron's palazzo, I had thought it might be better to call it all off and yet...could I tell Claire I couldn't do it? I would not fall short of audacity in my sister's eyes! That's why I brought her, I suppose, to keep me screwed to the sticking point. Such stupid things turn our days and rule our stars: I did not want her to call me a chicken, clucking wildly in the night. Yet the darkness around us seemed to leech into my bones and I shivered.

"Steady, Signora Shelley," Tita said as we reached the servant's door. He worked a key and opened it into a wane light from a candle in a sconce.

"I'm sorry to have included you in this nonsense," I said.

"I am not sorry, Signora."

He pointed down a dark hall that went from the servant's rooms and kitchens into the Hunt's apartments. He took a step another way, waving at a sleepy watchman...a boy, really, who suddenly emerged from an alcove, a lantern and a knife in hand. What dangers did Byron's house anticipate? Shelley and I had heard stories of assassins in the night, knives and poisons, but that sleepy boy made me believe them more than any tale. Tita stopped briefly and spoke to him in hushed tones. The boy ignored me, Tita's wave toward me enough: he returned to sleep. Tita retreated and I heard the door we came in softly click to.

The humiliation to follow in the story galls me. I slunk and groped through empty hallways and past kitchens until I found myself in Hunt's family's rooms. I felt like a fool—yet determined to be so! Along about the kitchens, a nursery rhyme started in my head, unbidden:

The Queen of Hearts she baked some tarts,

all on a summer's day.

The knave of hearts, he stole the hearts,

and took them clean away.

I repeated it dumbly to pass the slow, galling time. I arrived at last in the front parlor. I went to the front door alcove and unlocked the door to ready my escape. Claire gave a little scratch to let me know she was there and had heard me. Moretto, that great creature, snuffled under the door, smelling little Hunts, no doubt. My mind again ran in old rhymes:

Fee, fie, foe, funt!

I smell the blood of a little Hunt,

Be he alive or be he dead,

I'll chase him round his little bed!

I felt small and mean as a naughty child. My situation was ridiculous. If discovered, I would be shunned by the Hunts. What would Byron think? What did I think of myself?

I thought myself unstoppable. As unstoppable as lava flows.

By the light leaking through high grated windows, I saw the prize—waiting on the fireplace mantle, a box. Claire had suggested Hunt would put his ornament on the mantle: could it be that simple? I crossed the room silent as a rat. It was a wooden frame without elaboration. I opened the lid to find Trelawny's ragged satchel inside. I eased it out, afraid that somehow a mousetrap would snap on my eager fingers just as I took the cheese—or the tart—the heart—whatever word you like for the impossible thing! I was dizzy with what I was doing, so much so I almost missed the sound down a corridor to all the sleeping rooms.

Time to leave!

I clutched the bag to me and eased the lid of the box shut. I thought of the weight—rather, the lack of weight now, of the box. Someone might lift it and know the heart was gone without looking in. I groped along the mantle and my fingers found something about the right shape and weight. I opened the box lid and put it in, lowering the lid again just as someone creaked out of a room, and candlelight eased into view, dimly glowing on the walls. I glided toward the darker shadows of the front door alcove. Only then did I think: of course, Hunt would miss whatever I had taken from elsewhere on the mantle to put in the box…but I could not move now.

Everything paused and everything listened. We breathed together, every chair and cushion and rug, hearing a sound like an ocean surf in my ears with every respiration. I felt light-headed. Then the light down the corridor receded. A door swung to with a loud bang. I started, then opened the front door and slipped out, my prize gripped to my chest. I emerged in Byron's front hall with the grand staircase leading up to his apartments.

Claire waited with the mastiff, Moretto, who snuffled under my skirts as I pushed him away. I smiled at Claire, shaking the bag. The dog wagged it tail at me and demanded pats on the head.

"You did it!" she said in a loud whisper, exulting.

I moved away and motioned to her to follow. Quickly! All was well. We could return Moretto to his post at the top of the stairs.

Instead, Claire opened Hunt's door and pushed the beast in! The devil padded in, nose to the ground—fee, fie, foe funt!

"Claire!" I put my hand over my mouth. Honestly, it was so unexpected.

Claire rubbed her hands like a figure in a pantomime.

"Run!" she cried.

Outside, I looked up and down the street, Pisa's Lung'Arno, and saw no one but Tita, lounging without a care, and the dirty river, the Arno, running down a channel in the middle, whispering to itself as if in a dream. Tita signaled me from the bridge, then followed us home at a trot. He asked no questions when we arrived, breathless. Tita left us at the door and we collapsed laughing into the front room.

"Why!" I said. She would not respond so I tickled her.

She shrieked. We fell laughing to the floor.

"He deserved it!" She pushed my hands away.

We climbed up and sat slumped on the settee, catching our breath.

Catarina came in, her top pulled on inside out. We waved her back to bed.

"Can I see it?" Claire said.

My hands were still white-knuckled, clasping Trelawny's leather satchel. I hadn't looked—I had no doubts until that moment. I loosed the ties and nosed inside—there it was: the dark-sooted but unburned heart in all its mystery, couched in the soft leather folds of the purse.

Mine—my own still pounding heart beat in rhythm to the thought—mine, mine, mine!

I pushed the bag on to Claire's lap. She looked in at the thing.

"That's it?" She reached a finger in as if it might burn her, as if all the heat it endured still emanated from it. She tapped its hard crust.

"It was too pure," I said.

"Maybe," Claire said.

"He was too good."

Claire nodded, her curls moving about her face. "Yes," she said.

We told stories about Shelley then—how he used to love sleepless nights, and stories, and his high-pitched and affecting declamations of ancient poetry—how we ran from all the world's claims and strictures…and its sadness…with him beside us; we shared our store of him into the night until we trailed off to bed, holding each other up. Claire had been my rival for his attention. But now she was the only one who understood what I felt, things that would live with me and then die to be forgotten—the impossible everyday life with him, and the odd shifting dreams he lived in all the quiet hours that lay in the between spaces of what everyone thought of as everyday. I embraced Claire at her chamber door before dragging off toward my own bed.

I kissed my little Percy, my last remaining child, who did not even shift in his solid slumber. I changed into my shift and climbed under the covers. I hid Shelley's heart beneath my pillow.

18 August, Tre Pallazi, Pisa
(two days after the burning)

In the morning, Jane woke me early to tell me her news: she had spoken with Hunt; she had convinced him that I was a true wife to Shelley, his helpmeet; he had relented and agreed to give me the heart.

I immediately felt bad about the dog. Even though it wasn't my fault, I said in defense to myself—both judge and jury disagreed and clamored for justice. You loved it being done, I accused myself. You would have done it if you had had the vinegar. And it was true. I wondered what the morning brought the Hunts—or what little feet came wandering out first, woken by a snuffling at the door?

"I know what a surprise this is," Jane said, smiling prettily. Her long hair hung down, enhancing how slender and tall she was: such a pretty doll, even just risen from her bed. Her large almond-shaped eyes fixed on me; I must have had an expression of confusion and embarrassment on my face. "Don't worry. Come let us get dressed and get that heart for you!"

I dressed in a fog. Should I go ask Mrs. Mason for advice? I had tried to keep her out of it beyond what she had already done. Byron? I still think he might prove angry that I broke into his house—and Tita's involvement would keep me quiet. He must not be punished any more for helping me. Thinking perhaps I could get away from Jane for a few moments and return it, somehow, I put Trelawny's purse into a bag when I had finished dressing. One of the maids stopped in to help me with my hair and to finish my toilet.

I went upstairs to breakfast with Jane and Claire, who was laughing.

"I don't see what's so funny," Jane said, put out, as I walked into the dining room.

The sun was out, slanting through the veranda window to slash along the tiles.

I scowled at Claire, so eager to start trouble, leaving me with the mess—so usual for her! She shook her head at me, and motioned for me to sit. I ate without tasting my food. I cuddled my Percy to me. He had been up early playing with his toy boats. I shuddered at his choice of toys. He accepted my attentions with the carelessness of the very young—as if it would always be this way. I felt myself a doomed prisoner, ready for the guillotine. Why did I not control my worst instincts? I could not blame Claire for that, she only helped me effect my purposes. I insisted on larceny in the night! I would have the heart at any hazard! And Jane had gotten it by just asking....

But I didn't want it that way, I realized. I preferred my own ridiculous fashion—my skullduggery and mischief. I puzzled at my determination to go on in my own way when Jane's way was clearly easier, less fraught with hurt feelings and regret.

We gathered our outerwear, donning capes and hats for the sun. We rode in our open calash. The others chattered and I hardly noticed until Claire leaned in to whisper in my ear.

"You have it?" she hissed.

I nodded.

"No secrets," Jane said, in good spirits because of her successful efforts to reconcile her friends.

To Jane, Claire said, "just comfort for the nervous heart, Jane. Look at her! I think she is afraid your rapprochement with Hunt will not be as total as you think."

"Why not?" Jane said sweetly.

"He is an ass!" Claire said.

Jane tut-tutted.

"He only wants what's good for Shelley, too. He did not understand the depth of feeling of our Maie."

"He put our Maie through the wringer because he is a selfish, short-sighted bully."

I could not help but smile at Claire. I still half-wished she hadn't released the dog into Hunt's house. Did my way have to include the dog?

At Byron's Palazzo, Jane went in to announce our coming.

"Maybe we can try to switch it back in while Hunt is giving one of his long-winded diatribes," Claire said. "Just ask him about the state of modern poetry...."

We chuckled. I nodded. We would have to try.

Looking disconcerted, Jane returned with a letter and the box. I couldn't go in? I stammered out something, but it was incoherent even to me. I took the box. It was light. He had taken out what I had put in. Reluctantly, I took the letter. I was ready to go home, then, but the two others looked at me expectantly. I read the letter. If he wouldn't meet with me, I didn't want to read his letter. It was nonsense, fatuous and self-serving. He confirmed: he wouldn't meet with me—and he only returned the heart to keep the peace—and he thought I had been too cold with Shelley—but he had come to understand that I my feelings ran deep. He said nothing about my already having the heart. Had he promised to return it only to find it gone?

Claire looked at me with raised eyebrows. Jane smiled weakly. "Well?" she said.

"He says he's sorry," I said.

Claire snorted.

"Let's go," I said to the driver.

"Aren't you going to open the box," Jane said, bewildered.

I shook my head.

When I got home, I ran upstairs, throwing the letter on my desk, where I would ignore it until I needed extra blotting paper. I opened the box, and looked into its emptiness for a time. I carefully placed my husband's unburned heart back inside.

What happened to it then?

When I mentioned that I had it to Byron, he said, "I wish never to hear about it again." I resolved to tell Trelawney nothing. Ever after, Hunt and I pretended all was well. I would even live in the same house as his family when he and I both followed Byron to Genoa, before Byron went to Greece to die fighting for Greek independence.

When I went to Mrs. Mason and related everything to her, we sat in her garden with the box. But she never asked to see what lay inside. I thanked her for making a man of me. I promised I would write a story for her children.

Finally, I decided to be done with Hunt's box. I searched my desk for something to keep the heart in. I found extra pages to Adonais, Shelley's elegiac poem to poor Keats, the young poet who had died in Rome. I thought about the last lines....

I am borne darkly, fearfully afar;

Whilst burning through the inmost veil of Heaven

The soul of Adonais, like a star,

Beacons from the abode where the Eternal are.

"It is his own elegy," I said aloud. The verse reminded me of the last line of my monster book: "he was soon borne away by the waves, and lost in darkness and distance."

I took Shelley's heart in my hand. I threw the box toward the fire. It hit the wall and fell, to become kindling. I wrapped the heart in the poem and put the poem in my desk, in a bottom drawer. His heart drawn from the fire is but a stone, unrelenting. What of it?

What have I gained in recovering it? Self-regard. This was never about my husband, but about me. Now I watch every fire close, looking for something I know I will never find. I cannot help but peer into the shadows that curl round the light. His heart is still unrecked. But it is not all loss: an important point.

A curious thing: I am no longer sorry about the dog.

The

Journal

of

Sorrow

The Journal of Sorrow—
    Begun 1822
But for my Child it could not
    End too soon.

Mary Shelley's epigraph to her new journal
(2 October 1822)

The facts of the fatal journey are as follows. My Shelley and my dear Ned Williams sailed for Livorno on 1 July to meet our friends, the Hunts—Leigh and Marianne and their large brood of children— arrived fresh from England. They sailed in high spirits. Leigh Hunt had left editing his old magazine, *The Examiner*, resigning his post to his brother, to come to Italy and edit a new magazine, *The Liberal*, meant to shake the foundations of the English nation, or at least stir up a desire for justice. From Italy, things that could not be said would finally be said, and Hunt would be out of the reach of incarceration. Lord Byron had been lined up to support the enterprise financially— and all of us, Shelley, Byron, Hunt, and myself, were to write for it. Hunt, Marianne, and what Byron deemed their unholy litter of unruly children, were to live on the first floor of Byron's spacious house— Palazzo Lanfranchi, in Pisa.

I had not wanted Shelley to travel. I was still ill from a miscarriage on 16 June, some two weeks before he sailed. The event had begun with a terrible sigh, a deflation into death. I felt afterwards, in shame, as if I had done it to myself, willfully. As if I had been too self-concerned to notice dire warnings, not filled with enough fortitude to stay abed, insufficiently loving to nurture a baby to term. But what more could I have done? The blood came loose like a nightmare and I swooned, someone catching me; I slipped into blackness and out again into a timeless place of waiting without resolve.

Shelley sent for a doctor, but we lived so isolated at Casa Magni, our lonely villa over the sea along the Tuscan coast, that he would not arrive before I dwindled. Death sat on the veranda patiently, counting the waves rolling in under the house. They all thought and so did I that I was about to die. I did not think of Percy Florence, my last and only child, to my further guilt, except with a vague regret. I cared even less for anyone else, even Shelley. Would it have been better if I had died? But no, what would become of my poor babe? Better, on reflection, that I endure, with all my guilty thoughts.

As I waited to die from blood loss, the world seemed to hum, the sound vibrating out of the earth, shaking my bones uncomfortably— as if bees crawled inside me, circling round my bones. I was so ill that for seven hours I lay nearly lifeless—kept from fainting by brandy, vinegar, eau de Cologne, I know not what else—at length ice was brought to our solitude—it came before the doctor so Claire and Jane were afraid of using it but Shelley overruled them. I was laid in a tub full with ice. Shelley carried me there himself. There are experiences so intense they cannot be remembered. I only know the moment of immersion as a kind of preternatural clarity, not of this world of feeling but one of pure mind and no time; I felt something so beyond cold it plunged me to a deafening light—they say I screamed and opened my eyes wide but I neither heard nor saw anything. Shelley applied the ice unsparingly, leaving me in a long time, though the others complained and pleaded for me as I unfastened my mouth wide and wailed to wake mountains that have slept since the world first shook with earthquake deamons. The ice stopped my bleeding until the doctor came. Shelley saved my life but weeks before he died. The others had been, unknowingly, pleading for my death.

I awoke from that experience overwhelmed and inconsolable. I had yet to forgive Shelley for saving me when he sailed away; I would never finish mourning my new unborn baby. (Add the little one to the list of my dead, I thought, and I will spend my days in mourning until my purgatory is fulfilled.) I had been outwardly only irritable, at myself and anyone. Shelley went on living as if life mattered and I felt torn in half inside, and ashamed to be so angry. Did I ever come out of the icy bath, I wonder? Do I lie there still, shocked, blood frozen in my veins, screaming though I cannot hear it?

I relapsed when Shelley and Ned tried to sail to Livorno, collapsing in my weakness, losing blood again, dyeing the stones of our balcony over the sea. I raved—I begged for them not to sail. I did not think they would die; I thought I would. They postponed sailing—yet another way I killed my husband and my dear Ned. Had they sailed the first time, there would have been a different moment for their return, perhaps, and perhaps no storm waiting to catch them up in its embrace. But not until 1 July did they leave us, scudding away over the waves in their quick-flying boat *Ariel* (or the *Don Juan*, as Byron had insisted on christening it, though Shelley disliked the name).

When they left our home, I lay abed. I cried to watch him go. I said to him, "I wish I could break these chains and leave this dungeon." I meant my bed, the house, Italy, my body, this world…I don't know what all I meant. I can hardly repeat my own behavior now without galling shame. I sent a note to Hunt by mail, repeating my cry against the chains I saw all around me, entreating him to do I know not what about it. I did not know what he made of my entreaties until sometime later. Like everything else I have accomplished, it did me no good.

But none of this matters—it is only what happened, the chain that binds us each to circumstance and chance. It is only true. He drowned and I passed a time I cannot describe. Some stories cannot be told but as fragments, as dreams, fits. In them, I know my Shelley again. What of that? Life is but a dream. Death but another kind of life. So my Shelley believed. Here, take these fallen things, I hold them out to you—dead leaves to quicken some new birth....

Fit the First

Above Shelley's boat, his Ariel, *low clouds sagged and darkness smeared like ink down a page, dripping into the waiting sea.*

"We shouldn't have sailed," Ned shouted to no one. He turned his face from the wet. "We must turn back."

The vessel had only left anchor and rounded out of the safe harbor of Livorno a few minutes since, heading into the open sea, yet already the shore was lost in darkness and distance.

"Maie is expecting us," Shelley shouted to his fate. The wind seemed to reply, but what it had to say, though loud, was lost in incoherence.

The men worked with purpose, but would not hurry—not yet. They did not truly worry at first, when they might have saved themselves. Instead, they paused to consider the storm and which way it would move. Ned lifted his loose, wet shirt, as he rubbed a hand on his chest while looking out to sea. Shelley pulled his nankeen trousers from sticking to his legs; skinny, he resembled a cat caught in a downpour, its fur matted ridiculously to reveal the scrawny thing beneath. The two men shrugged at one another, turned to the tasks of sailing.

"I am expected as well," Ned said, not loudly enough to be heard. It didn't matter.

The rain hardened. Quickly, the water on deck thickened, deepened. Much more than expected. The men exchanged looks of shared alarm, at last. For a time the two struggled in feverish haste with the craft, turning her across or through the waves, letting her run too fast with the wind, slipping further out to sea. They worked in silence with each other, surrounded by bluster and motion—deafening and unbalanced—a sea in turmoil. Waves spread out on the deck from one side, then another, then seemly on all sides together.

Shelley stopped and looked out, as if he could see a light in the distance. He hung out from the rigging with his arms above his head.

Ned shouted, "it will pass but not yet. Keep at it!"

The rain, the wind, increased, changing direction continuously. Shelley's hair rose up freely, seemed to take light and electricity, sparking; his shirt billowed despite being soaked in the driving winds. His wide eyes, large and preternaturally blue, looked unblinking into the storm. He seemed to see in it some symbol of his own self. I am a bark, he thought, in the storm.

"But I am needed," he said simply.

Somehow Ned heard him, or guessed at what to say. "She'll get nothing if you don't help me. Which way to shore—which way?"

Ned was crying though he did not stop struggling with their overborne craft. His tears only added to the falling rain.

"You can sail without me," Shelley said. "Better without...."

"No," Ned shouted. He pulled too hard, in his frustration, on the ropes, pulling the sails around. The vessel shook uncertainly, losing momentum.

"Too wide," Shelley said, no longer helping, "the world too wide in misery—and cold—"

"We have to drop the sails," Ned shouted, "we should have already; it was a fool's game to try to outrace the wind."

Shelley slipped like water off the deck into the sea. His splash made no difference in the upheavals of the insatiable sea. Crying out, Ned released the ropes and the boat floundered, spinning free. It rocked and swamped. It sank, like Shelley, with alacrity. Ned struggled to remove his boots.

"Shelley!" he cried, a lament.

He took off his shirt. The water overtook him. He worked his arms and kicked.

"Shelley!" he cried.

The storm, sensing its moment, intensified, fingers grasping as wind and wave, pulling at his clothes, smearing his vision.

"Which way," he said, not so much swimming as flailing toward uncertain darkness, "which way?—Shelley!"

As sometimes happens, misery proved too wide for either.

Fit the Second

Out at sea, a storm—the wind its herald, the clouds its dark flag unfurled—declared its mastery.

"More life!" Shelley shouted, leaning out.

"Bollocks, Shelley," Ned said, without rancor.

Shelley stood casually in the bow of the Ariel, *watching, with a frown, as the storm moved toward them, casual itself, like a stray thought of destruction, ponderous but inevitable. Or perhaps the storm would turn aside? Would it swallow them without malice or forethought or vanish into the empyrean? Would it be better to stay here or be taken there? Shelley smiled at fate. His shirt rippled and his hair flew up like the spray against the shore. He whooped, feeling light. He imagined he and fate were companionably indifferent together. It was too late, he could see, and all had been decided— however it had been decided.*

Ned was dressed more warmly with his short sailing jacket and sailor's knit cap tight over his brow. He was larger and more imposing than his friend the poet, but frantic as opposed to Shelley's calm. One was the passing storm, the other encompassed the patient sky.

Shelley tilted his head back, drops of rain touching his face; he held tight, swaying with the waves. Ned bellowed with frustration.

Ned looked back toward where the shore had been. All was lost in mist and distance. How far out were they? The ship had but just sailed out of sight of the harbor at Livorno. Ned worked alone to turn the ship—their Ariel, *tame spirit of the wind—to the south, away from the storm.*

"Prospero, too, made such a storm," Shelley shouted, "and Ariel saw all through safely at the wizard's command. I will tell our Ariel to bring us to a magic isle! Safe and dry!"

There had been other boats around them when they set out. But now all the fishermen in their feluccas were lost in mist or had turned back for harbor. One of them had called to them, something incoherent, and motioned for them to follow. They had sailed on into smoke on the water and rising waves.

"There's still time," Ned called, his voice seeming far away, the words ripped by the wind.

"We will make it," Shelley called, *"or we won't."*

Ned worked the craft with increasing urgency. The storm crowded up behind them. The Ariel began to take water. The storm pounced like a cat when a mouse scurries out from its safe hole. Now it would play with its prey, building an appetite.

Shelley, holding the lines tight, leaned out over the waves again. He breathed in a pure serene. The salt smell drenched him; hard grains of it collected behind his neck itchily as the rain washed the sea salt and sweat from his hair; he scratched as he swayed over the waves reaching up: they grasped at him with fingers of spray and sputum.

Ned ran up to him again, held his arm.

"We'll have to swim for it."

"I can't swim," Shelley said lightly.

"Damn, I know–I'll hold you, we'll head in."

"No."

"Shelley, this is...this is it," he said lamely.

Shelley nodded. Suddenly his eyes seemed to focus on his friend.

"I should have helped you turn about," he said softly. Then more loudly, directly in his friend's ear, he said: *"Trelawny once tried to teach me to swim, you know, in a deep pool in the woods behind the*

house. What I learned was how to let all the air out of my lungs to sink to the bottom. I sat like an Eastern mystic on a lotus. I would have died then if he hadn't pulled me out. I think he knew I'd rather he hadn't done it, 'but what would Mary have said,' he asked me...."

"There's not time for stories!"

Ned was crying; Shelley hugged him close.

"There's no time at all, for anything else."

The ship swamped fast, sailing once more over a large wave but then dipping in the trough, sailing under and into the next wave, tossing the men over into the sea. Ned called out in surprise and fear, a banshee wail. He swam, first looking about, unsure even where the shore might be, then turning, doomed, to try his strength, to head anywhere without giving up.

Below, the darkness and water took the wide-eyed and the fish-mouthed, arms open in embrace of what had come; they kissed his eyes to sleep and, stripping him of his flowing clothes, placed him carefully among their treasures, by sunken hulls and cannon balls, skulls and coral, for slinking bottom-dwellers among the oozy woods to come and pluck out his eyes, having other uses for such things in the cold and quiet at the bottom of the sea.

After a time, gentle Ned was brought and placed lovingly beside his friend, both naked, shriveled and in sweet repose, together always.

Fit the Third

Eyes in the water.

Shelley stood at the prow, looking out. With hands pointing, clenching, waving. Water spouts rose and waves crashed together and the sea tottered and spumed.

"Awake!" Shelley shouted.

Ned cried out, but the wind threw his words into the waves. The Ariel stopped in centerpoint, seemed to rise out of the sea, coming up and about as if raised on a winch.

Shelley held up both hands. For a moment the waves paused mid-crashing; the wind inhaled between blow; the clouds, puffing up and grimacing in the sky, held. All held as if on puppet strings for the show to begin. Shelley glanced back a moment, his clothes, wet through, clung to him, dripping. His open collar had been blown askew until his thin chest shone, slick with sputum. His wide, pale face glowed, almost translucent, the green veins in his forehead standing out through marble white. His hair was alive like medusa's above and around his head. A halo for the damned.

"Jump," Shelley said to Ned, with a smile, "jump now. It will not hold but a moment."

All held its breath still, impossibly. The clouds turned expectantly, slowly, waiting.

But Ned paused to say, "fuck?"

He looked out and saw it—them?—too. Did he? Eyes in the water. And tentacled arms waving and slipping under the waves. A sailor's nightmare from the depths. Brought by the storm? Bringing the storm?

Shelley's hands shook, bending fingers back painfully. The storm crashed, raged, shook. The noise shattered, shouted, rumbled. The water began to spin in a maelstrom. Shelley placed his legs wide apart, gyrated his arms, trying to keep balance. A great whirlpool opened, gaping down deep into the ocean, revealing a dark, scurrying, churning heart of water, compressing and tearing terrifically; the boat, held its place until, almost vertical, it scudded down the side of the whirlpool, descending into the depths.

Ned leapt, but that moment had firmly passed.

The boat sped up, plummeted with sickening speed, until even Shelley fell across the deck; nearly sideways, the boat ribboned down the rushing walls of the whirlpool, arrived at the churning bottom still dropping away toward the ocean floor; spinning like a top for a moment on the unsteady mass of water tumbling and shuttering, the Ariel *suddenly pulled below the waves, shooting, like a cannon ball fired straight down, beneath the bottom of the sea.*

The last sound before the water closed over them was a moan, a cry of the waves, in joy.

The whirlpool collapsed on itself, clapping to with delight. The storm lost interest in its fury, seemed to wander off—the clouds broke up, like an audience drifting away through the streets after the show has ended, whispering of wonders, exhausted but content.

Eyes shut for sleep. Tentacles rested in loving embrace of precious things lost to the world above.

Fit the Fourth

Ned's brown eyes, intent, watched the storm clouds approaching too fast. The sky above them deepened, dark shapes forming in clear blue.

"It didn't turn aside, Shelley," he said quietly.

Ned directed the Ariel *through the low choppy waves. They had set sail in sunlight; a dark squall on the horizon had shown itself; they had thought it would pass on and take no notice of them; they had thought it would stall and dissipate out to sea; they had thought it would move too slowly to bother them; instead, the clouds overtook them, increasing in intensity.*

"They may yet miss us—or pass quickly," Ned said, without conviction. Fat drops tapped his head, as if to ridicule him.

"The clouds are not the only ones following us," Shelley said from the stern, a glass to his eye as he gazed backward.

Shelley rose unsteadily to his feet to hand the instrument to his friend. Shelley had a sunken chest, and stooped slightly, but displayed an easy manner, as if lounging, not weighed down with the world; he smiled wanly as the taller man took the spyglass and trained it where Shelley's thin, delicate finger showed him another dark shape on the horizon. Behind them. Shelley took direction of their boat as Ned gazed.

"What the devil? Are they to be caught in this, too? Are there more fools like us?"

"They are following us," Shelley said.

Ned lowered the glass. "You're mad," he said. "It won't pass us by," he said, meaning the storm, cloaking the sky ever darker.

"We'll run with the wind," Shelley said.

"All right," Ned said, "or drown in the attempt."

The two men clasped hands a moment, springing to tie the ropes or work the sails.

"If the storm is too hard we will have to be ready to lower the sails fast. Be ready."

Shelley laughed.

"I'm always ready," he said. "They're gaining on us."

The ship behind them was heading distinctly toward them. Rain began to fall harder; the winds shifted and shifted again, helter skelter.

"The storm will take them, too—what could pirates want in such weather?" Ned wondered.

"Maybe they are not pirates at all," Shelley said easily.

"It's too late to warn us."

"Yes, it is."

The storm took them all up. It turned and tottered them, but they withstood. The ship behind had been lost as mist obscured their vision, but soon reappeared, closer now. The men aboard worked hard to keep their vessel afloat, but also to close the distance with the Ariel. *The men of the other boat looked intently at them—to what purpose? A rogue wave shook them all—much taller, faster, unexpectedly rising over them and pushing through. As it subsided, Shelley laughed at the surprise of it. The storm bore down again as if in response.*

The other boat drew beside them. The men gestured at them, angry, importuning.

"I recognize one of these men," Shelley said. "Ignore them."

"What could they mean?" Ned said, despairing.

Shelley thought of his wife and child; and then he thought of nothing; his thoughts were the wind.

Fit the Fifth

Shelley refused the storm, intent on reading poetry. The rain pattered on the leaves, staining the words clear. He shook the book out to dry it. He leaned over it to shield it with his body. He read:

Why am I not as are the dead,

Since to a woe like this I have been led

Through the dark earth, and through the wondrous sea?

"Yes," he said, enchanted by the words of the young poet, "the wondrous sea."

Shelley held the book open, balanced in one hand. He noticed, only now, that his neck hurt; his eyes strained against increasing darkness; only his other hand, unconsciously tight on the boat's edge, kept him from falling to be swallowed up by the water. He read on:

Goddess! I love thee not the less: from thee

By Juno's smile I turn not—no, no, no—

While the great waters are at ebb and flow.—

I have a triple soul! O fond pretense—

For both, for both my love is so immense,

I feel my heart is cut in twain for them.

"My heart, too," he said to the dead poet, "is cut in twain...for all who love me."

An answering voice came to him over the rocking sea, over the holler of wind, over the creaking of the Ariel *as it grasped itself together still by joint and screw. He read on:*

And so he groan'd, as one by beauty slain.

Shelley looked up, surprised by the young man, small and neatly dressed in a comfortable, dry brown English jacket and trousers, as if out on holiday in the countryside, climbing in over the side of the moving boat, the boat still caught in a sudden squall.

"Hello?" Shelley said. "What's this?"

"I thought my name was the one writ on water," the small man said, taking hold of the rigging to keep himself upright and on board.

Shelley laughed. He took his copy of Keats' Endymion, *and turned the pages over backwards on the spine in his haste, shoving it in his pocket where it would not be lost.*

"And I always thought you were taller...when I only knew your poems," Shelley said. "Good to see you again, my friend."

His right hand holding the side of the boat, he extended his left; Keats with his right on the rigging, extended his left as well and they shook off hands awkwardly.

"I'm sorry you didn't come up from Rome to see us," Shelley said, "before the curtain dropped."

The storm, as if frustrated by their disregard, rocked the boat with more force, a child who will have its way—will have it! But what can a storm threaten when all is said and done? When all is given up already, O death, where is thy sting?

"I couldn't," the young man said, "not just because I was ill: you were too wild in the sun for me, you know." The young man looked out at sea a moment. "It seemed to matter then. I needed the shade of beechen green."

"You were most welcome," Shelley said.

"And you are most welcome now, to where I dwell."

"Ah," Shelley said, "we're dead then?"

"Finally," John Keats said.

"Yes, finally."

"But I think you're being followed," Keats said, pointing off.

Shelley looked back. There was a bark spinning on the waves. There the storm continued, but here: the storm seemed to have abated suddenly.

"Ah, I think that's my boat—the Ariel. *Still struggling. Am I still there? What do you think that's supposed to mean?"*

"Oh, Gods," Keats said, "you mean we still have to answer questions like that?"

"Maybe it's all mystery now. All poetry."

"It was all mystery, then."

Shelley looked to the horizon; it was all around.

"Perhaps I'm mistaken."

Keats sat heavily.

"You know," he said, "I figured there would be no poems here, honestly. I thought those were for mortality—an aching after immortality."

"Well, have you actually tried writing any poetry here?"

Keats laughed.

"Well, no…."

The light had a peculiar quality of leeching into the darkness like ink spilled across a page of verse. What words, thought Shelley, have I for all this?

"All the words we have need of," said Keats, taking hold of Shelley's hand again. "And more. We have time now to talk, if you like."

Shelley felt some clarity, some recognition that he might be underwater. Not that it mattered. After all, he couldn't swim. No need to worry about struggling.

"Do we have all the time in the world then?" he said, airily.

"No, no, no," said Keats' voice, "but time enough."

Shelley could still feel the pressure of the other's hand, cold though it was.

"Then," said Shelley, his own voice sounding to himself like water rushing past tree roots, over rocks, into a pond he had seen but lost somewhere beyond recall, "I have some questions."

"I will answer," said John Keats, affably. "Everything...that I know."

"Which isn't much."

"No, I know."

There was a pause.

"Then I propose," Shelley said, "that we have a poetry contest instead."

Keats laughed.

"That's a fantastic idea. Do you have pen, ink, and paper?"

They looked about themselves and found everything they needed, arranged themselves with space to write, facing toward one another, comfortably companionable, and set to work. Scratch, scratch, scratch. They wrote poetry down below the bottom of the sea, somewhere over the cold hill's side, safe behind the scattered stars, out beyond the fields we know. Not a word fell out of place. Not a rhyme was lost. Not a rhythm faltered. And nothing slid away from the tip of the tongue to frustrate or bebother. Everything at last was exquisitely fitted.

Fit the Sixth

"Tack there, Ned," Shelley said. "Ned, tack! Tack!"

Ned grinned at him. "Aye, aye, Cap'n. Luf! Look at you, like you know what you're doing?" Ned laughed "You're a wonder, my friend, but no sailor."

"We're not on open sea," Shelley said. "I know this dream—I know this place."

The storm shook and spun round them. In the clouds fluttered a scattering of wings. Strange things flew, singing. Lightening flashing up and down, running like ladders to the waiting sky. A wailing and music came over the wind.

"I know," Ned said, sobered, "I know, but it feels like—"

"Keep on now, Ned—we're going to make it. Tack, damn your eyes!"

Shelley clapped Ned on the shoulder, but Ned only looked out over the sea.

"Where to?" Ned asked.

"Out, Ned! Further! We're not lost. Not yet. We need to be further out! Then we will be well and truly lost!"

"How long will…?"

"No time. No time at all."

Safe ashore, I watched them through my spyglass until I lost them in the glare of endless sky and spinning diamonds of dazzling sunlight. I was blinded, watching them leave me to sail into the uncharted depths of a dream.

Fit the Seventh

The boat overcame them with the storm. Larger, faster, it bore down. Shelley leaned out from the Ariel, *watching. Would the storm push the vessels apart, or would the other arrive at its target? A man cloaked in black stood unmoving in the prow, returning Shelley's stare as the other men on the boat worked furiously to keep her afloat. The man had eyes like dark pools, lightless but intense. The wind buffeted them all.*

"What the devil are they doing?" Ned cried to Shelley. "Turn off, you'll hit us!" he shouted at the other boat.

The waves tossed in the wind; shadows drew down the clouds. Spraying, darkling, biting, the storm worried them, circled them.

"They're coming too close," Ned cried.

"They're after me," Shelley said, too quiet for his friend to hear.

The boat had no markings they could make out.

The man in black on the boat watched fearlessly. Shelley smiled, also fearless.

"Is that death? Is that death-in-life and death," Shelley murmured. "Are they dicing for our souls?"

"For what crimes?" Shelley yelled.

The man stirred. "Am I a jury," the man shouted back. It was not a question.

The storm judged them all, with wind and fury.

All were found wanting. But some the sea tossed back. Some the storm claimed, washed up on unimaginable shores.

Fit the Eighth

After the storm, calm: but for the two delirious men, clasping each other, clinging to the masts of a boat with sails hastily drawn down, torn and puddled at their feet; the men shouted for joy and performed a robust but awkward sailor's jig, kicking their legs with abandon and stamping their feet. The storm that threatened their lives receded to the South. Behind it, the water spread calm and emerald as if nothing would ever disturb it again.

"We live," Ned shouted. "Live!"

Shelley crowed in delight, his hands rounding his mouth to shape his cry.

"I couldn't see my hand in the spray," Shelley said, holding it out like a wonder. "Not in front of my face. The deck looked already underwater, the rain collapsed so fast."

The men laughed, though no joke had been told.

"Hey, there," Ned called to another boat that had been trapped in the squall—they, too, had been trying to outrun the storm on the edge of its leading gale. "You're too close."

The other vessel approached unabated.

"Hey, hey, hey," Ned said, waving his hands out now.

The men on the other boat, four fisherman damp in their ragged, dark shirts and short sailor pants, came on.

"We are blessed men," Shelley yelled to them, leaning out from the rigging, "all of us."

The men evidently argued among themselves, sullen and snappish, gesturing. The man at the helm steered her implacably on—dangerously close to the Ariel.

"English Lords," one said, in low Italian, "throw the money chest."

"They think we're Byron," Shelley said, laughing.

"They don't care who we are," Ned said. "I'll get a pistol and clear up their confusion."

Shelley threw up a hand to say, "go ahead."

The other vessel swung around the Ariel, *as if trying to corral her, the men on board still arguing. Ned made his way toward the supplies.*

"Look out there," Shelley said to Ned, as the other boat lurched in suddenly, ramming the Ariel *in the stern.*

The men on both ships fell, though all stayed aboard their vessels. The other boat, rocking unsteadily, drifted back.

"You've done for us," Ned shouted, no longer looking for his gun. "Take us with you, or we'll perish!"

The men never stopped arguing: one looked angry, two looked frightened, the last remained sullen, as if content to say by his demeanor, "there, I told you so—it would not work!" They were all of them useless, paying no attention now to the Ariel, *sinking faster, as they bickered. They drifted back further in recoil from the impact. The angry man began to yell loudly, to gesture vehemently.*

Ned opened their money chest and threw over a handful of coins, trying to get their attention.

"No," Ned shouted, as the other vessel continued to recede.

"The lazaretto,*" Shelley said.*

"Hardly big enough," Ned said.

"We will float beside it, and hold on."

He unstrapped the little boat from its mooring. The men quickly left the Ariel *as it listed, backwards; soon the tipping would precipitate faster and the entire boat would vanish from the surface. The other vessel turned and headed, unevenly—the sailors on it still shouting at one another—back toward Livorno.*

Bobbing beside the lazaretto, *clutching the side because he could not swim, Shelley said, "it's a great day to be alive."*

"Always a fine day to be with you, dear Shelley," Ned said.

The men began to kick their legs, pushing the skiff on over a profound sea. But the horizon opened forever without a shore.

Fit the Ninth

Even before sailing, Shelley marked the men in the felucca watching. They blended in with all the other fishermen preparing to sail—but proved too curious by half. Four men, crouching and working with ropes to no purpose—eyes intent on the Englishmen.

The harbormaster had stopped them before they could set out, or rather, had stopped Trelawney, who was about to accompany them out to sea on the Bolivar, *Byron's boat. Trelawney tried to ignore him, or shrug and feign he did not understand, but that only made things worse. The harbormaster stood unsteadily in his craft, backed by two slovenly Italian soldiers arguing over a last bit of shared tobacco, and intensified his argument with Trelawny, demanding more papers, kinds that Shelley had never heard of; when Trelawny, leaning out from the* Bolivar, *replied, arms wide, pleading to sail, the harbormaster only looked away, making a show of not listening. This wasn't going to end well.*

"They think to baffle us," Shelley said to Ned.

Ned raised his eyebrows, looking first at the soldiers but then following Shelley's gaze to the fishermen.

"Them again," he said.

"Yes," Shelley said. "I think they have arranged for us to lose our escort. We'll have to outrun them."

"Again," Ned said. "But there's a storm coming."

"We'll beat it out, too—they'll hesitate."

"We'd be fools to go out in it."

"So would they," Shelley said.

Fit the Tenth

Albe intentionally fired wide, simply requesting by that extreme means Shelley's attention.

The Bolivar *maintained its position alongside the* Ariel.

"I won't miss again," Byron said. He retrieved another pistol.

Shelley sighed theatrically and closed his Keats, turning the spine backwards, shoving it in his pocket.

"Then shoot," he said. "Shoot, Albe."

There was no one else on either vessel. There was no one in the active world. Everything was empty. The moon, slowly falling from the sky, loomed huge above them, the end of the world nigh. Had the world slipped its moorings and sailed into the darkness? The sea stormed but no clouds were visible. The sun was retreating in space. Soon all would be cold and lifeless.

Byron fired.

Shelley bent over at the impact. But the pistol ball could not enter his inviolable heart, unassailable stone to outlast eternity beyond the end of the world. The shot glanced off, plunking on the deck, rolling there, slightly bloodied, leaving red trails, following the erratic movement of the deck in the heaving waves.

"Try again," Shelley said encouragingly, dabbing fitfully at the shallow wound above his heart.

Fit the Eleventh

What if I had dragged his corpse from the waves and brought his body in a sealed box to my room—to my very own workshop of filthy creation? What if I had remade my Shelley anew, stitched of better stuff than ever he had been made before? Could I not take the dead matter and infuse life, like my student of unhallowed arts?

But why stop there? Why could I not take everything back to nothing, and start again? Return the world by earthquake to its roots?

Until gray. All gray.

All fog.

All winter.

All set to nothing. Then think! *The* Ariel *did not sail. My dear men did not drown. Or get shot. Their ship, never built. None spoke of sailing; none drew ill-fated designs for boats in the sands at Casa Magni. For they did not live. They were never born.*

People did not come to dominate the land. The land did not rise, buckle, scarred and riven, into mountains. The old great lizards did not walk the earth. The oceans never receded.

All gray.

Endless sea.

Not a drop to drink…for no drinker to drink it.

Silence. I could be still. At last. All I needed to do was tear all to pieces. It sounded glorious.

So I could be at peace, in a peace that will not last as the tide turns again and the world begins anew. Motion and time, again. And all as it must be—all exactly as before, nothing, not the wash of the least wave or the breath of the faintest wind, the least out of place.

And I bereft, as I must be. And always will.

What use dreams?

When the men sailed, I bided anxiously over Percy Florence, my babe, and did not think about losing Shelley. I thought, on his return, I would resolve to be happy. Instead, a dark time between us, better forgotten, will be etched in memory: my last moments with my husband were desperate pleadings; my last communications, bitterness.

Shelley and I exchanged a handful of letters in the days before his death. From me, came pleas and recriminations; from him came cool replies saying he had obtained necessaries for our home. I begged him to come and take me away from the oppressive loneliness that I knew he cherished at Casa Magni, tucked in an out of the way corner of Tuscany; he entreated me to humor him and stay on through the Summer, and perhaps beyond. I do not like to think what damage I had done with those letters, but do not know if I could have helped writing them.

Shelley and Ned sailed and stayed a week, rejoicing to see the Hunts at Livorno, conferring with Byron at Pisa, and doing business. From their letters, we expected them on Monday, 8 July. Jane had had a letter from her Edward, our Ned, dated Saturday, in which he said that he waited for Shelley who was still at Pisa. He wrote that Shelley's return was certain, "but" he continued, "if he should not come by Monday, I will come in a felucca and you may expect me Tuesday evening at the furthest." That was Monday, the fatal Monday, but with us it was stormy all day and we did not at all suppose that they could put to sea—that day we laughed and shuddered at our madmen and declared that two madmen cancelled each other out and surely they would not sail in a storm!

Twelve at night we had a stronger thunderstorm. Tuesday it rained all day, but was calm. The sky wept on their graves, but we did not know it. We spoke of them, longed for them, made a game of waiting for them and praising them, each in turn. On Wednesday, the wind was fair from Livorno and in the evening several feluccas arrived thence. We hailed them for news. One brought word that our men had sailed on Monday, but we did not believe them.

Thursday was another day of fair wind and we said today, truly. It became a magic phrase—"truly, today"—and we waited up late, not wanting the day to pass. When twelve at night came and we did not see the tall sails of the little boat double the promontory before us we began to fear not the truth but some illness—some disagreeable news about their detention. We would not name what we feared. We grew agitated, our jokes thinner, our praise of our men more desperate. The night wind blew until it seemed to fill our minds and we could not think for it. We stayed up all night. An airy feeling took us up, we felt unable to focus. A haunting by the unthinkable kept us not thinking, always thinking. Jane wrought herself up hard and fine like a string on her guitar, turned until it would break; she sang absently, unable to finish a phrase or hear a word spoken as she listened for the sound of our lost ones sailing home, hailing us off the water, torches and lanterns alight, excusing themselves with apology and with prizes from their journey.

The next day, a day of heavy sea and bad wind, our waiting changed to desperate action. Jane would have had herself sailed across the bay immediately, the only way for us to leave Casa Magni and start for Pisa, then on to Livorno, if necessary, but the weather rebuffed her. I wished her to wait for letters; Friday is mail day. As sailing was denied to her, Jane resolved to have herself rowed, but the swell rose so that no boat would venture out. At noon, that Friday, 12 July, our letters came—our first true intimation of disaster. Then came the letter from Leigh Hunt to Shelley that said "pray write to tell us how you got home, for they say that you had bad weather after you sailed Monday and we are anxious." I read the letter to Jane; I could not stop shaking. The letter dropped from my hand.

I recited it over a second time, in a hollow voice, already from memory.

"Pray write to tell us how you got home, for they say that you had bad weather after you sailed Monday and we are anxious."

I thought, for a moment, I would never read another sentence. Or ever dream again. But words are my life and dreams my unceasing companions. The words pry my dreams from me, whatever I will. They make the story. What must I do? I lay them before you . They weave a tapestry of my sorrow. And I offer you yet one more useless thing, a flotsam of the deep.

Fit the Twelfth

I awoke and found myself floating. I had been sleeping, my head resting on his lap.

"I...my dearest Shelley."

I looked up at his wide pale eyes. He looked to the far horizon.

"I had a dream." My eyes clouded, blurred with tears. "A storm. All lost."

He smiled, but still gazed out at the shoreless sea.

"And were we washed ashore with Caliban? or like Viola?" he said, not looking at me. "Did we have wonderful adventures—were their spirits flying in the air and beautiful sounds?"

We glided over water, rising and falling like the bounce of a bough bent low to the ground with children riding it on a summer's lark.

"No," I said, "in my dream, you—or did you?"

Did he kill himself? Was he murdered? Was it only chance?

My thoughts clouded. I wanted him to look at me. He looked at me.

"Tell me quick, love," he said, "are your eyes brown or blue, my sweet Maie?"

I mazed at him, then smiled. It was an old stratagem for teasing me.

"Both. You know this. Both. Depends on light and mood and chance."

We slid away over water. His wide eyes looked straight through me, seemed to see the sea below the craft and there envision strange treasures and tentacled depths.

Behind him I saw the unfettered sky. I knew no end to it, looking up at him.

"So what did you see in your dream?" he said.

"It was only a dream," I said, "not real."

"Ah…both," he said, smiling with a frown. "You know that. Both."

About the Author

Dr. David Sandner is a member of the HWA and SFWA. Recent work includes novella books *Mingus Fingers* (2019) and *Hellhounds* (2022), from Fairwood Press, co-written with Jacob Weisman. *The Afterlife of Frankenstein* (2023) is due out in November in Lanternfish's Clockwork Editions series. His short stories and poems appear in leading magazines, including *Asimov's SF, Weird Tales, PodCastle*, and in anthologies, like the *HWA Poetry Showcase VI, The Mammoth Book of Dark Magic, Monstroddities, D.O.A III*, and others. He has published scholarship on Mary Shelley, Philip K. Dick, horror, the critical history of the fantastic, science fiction, and the workings of the sublime. He is a Professor of English at California State University, Fullerton.